BIR

Books should be returned or renewed by the last
date above. Renew by phone **03000 41 31 31** or
online *www.kent.gov.uk/libs*

With special thanks to Tom Easton

To Theo

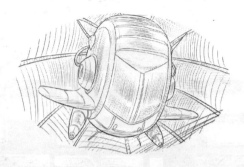

ORCHARD BOOKS

First published in Great Britain in 2016 by The Watts Publishing Group

1 3 5 7 9 10 8 6 4 2

Text © 2016 Beast Quest Limited.
Cover and inside illustrations by Artful Doodlers with special thanks to Bob and Justin
© Orchard Books 2016

Series created by Beast Quest Limited, London

The moral rights of the author and illustrator have been asserted.

A CIP catalogue record for this book is available from the British Library.

ISBN 978 1 40834 064 6

Printed in Great Britain

MIX
Paper from
responsible sources
FSC® C104740

The paper and board used in this book are made from wood from responsible sources

Orchard Books
An imprint of Hachette Children's Group
Part of The Watts Publishing Group Limited
Carmelite House, 50 Victoria Embankment, London EC4Y 0DZ

An Hachette UK Company
www.hachette.co.uk
www.hachettechildrens.co.uk

VELOTH
THE VAMPIRE SQUID

BY ADAM BLADE

ORCHARD

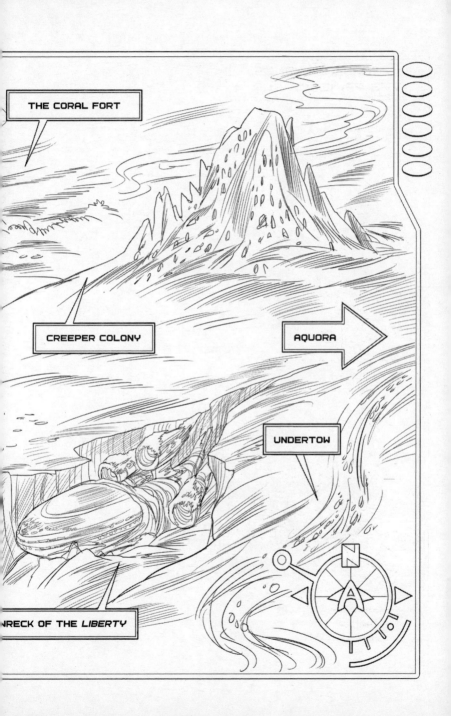

>TRANSMISSION FROM THE STARSHIP
LIBERTY

Any who threaten the SS *Liberty*
must die.

For 2,000 years I have lain at the
bottom of the ocean, forgotten.
For 2,000 years I have guarded my
ship. But my duty will never end:
analyse, react, destroy. Time may
have corroded my circuits, but I
have only grown more determined.

Now I have built four weapons to
aid me in my mission — creations
so powerful, nothing can stand
in their way. Enemies of the SS
Liberty beware. I will never stop
hunting you.

All threats must be terminated!

CHAPTER ONE

BLACKOUT!

Max twisted the wheel of his new sail sub as it passed the marker buoy, which glowed pink in the Aquoran evening. The vessel tipped sharply and Max had to lean backwards out over the edge to keep it balanced. His head missed the buoy by mere inches but he needed to take some risks if he was going to catch up with Lia.

He looked up to see his friend briefly break the surface of the water before diving back under, hardly causing a ripple. She was well ahead of him and increasing the gap. Max was starting to regret challenging her to a race, especially before he'd had a chance to get used to the sail sub's controls. But he'd been so excited about trying out the clever new design that he couldn't wait. The vessel's hull was the size of a large Aquoran car and was shaped like a slightly flattened egg when viewed from the side. It had a small cockpit, fins for control and a retractable keel which was used when the sail sub was on the surface.

A sudden, fierce gust of wind gave Max some hope and he pulled in the mainsail to take advantage of it. The sail sub leapt ahead as if it had been stung and Max saw that he was gaining on Lia. There was still just enough sunlight left for him to see her sleek shape racing under the surface, her webbed feet kicking her along.

I'm catching up with her!

But then Lia turned over on to her back, grinning. Max was confused, until the Merryn girl gave him a wave, kicking hard and shooting ahead at what seemed like double speed. The next moment the wind changed and the sail sub slowed to a crawl.

"Try the spinnaker, Max," a voice crackled in his earpiece. It was Niobe, Max's mother. He could just make her out, watching from the dock, silhouetted against the blazing harbour lights. "The wind should be directly behind you now."

Max didn't need telling twice. He flipped a switch on the console and felt the clunk and grind of the shimmering sail unfurling at the very front of the sail sub. It was made from a lightweight metal fabric and caught the breeze instantly. The sail strained forward, hauling the vessel along behind.

Lia didn't seem bothered. She was toying

with him now, flitting back and forth around the vessel. Max gritted his teeth in frustration. "So that's the spinnaker, is it?" Lia said via Max's headset. "Very pretty. But you can't catch me, however many sails you use." She streaked ahead past the next glowing buoy. Lia was just too fast, and getting faster.

Wind power is great, Max thought, *but it can't beat a big turbo engine.* He looked down to a large red button on the control panel. He shrugged and slammed his fist down on it. *It's cheating, but only a little!*

A plexiglass canopy slid out and enclosed the cockpit as the keel retracted and the two sails folded back into the craft's body, locking themselves away in neat compartments. Max felt a thrill at the rumble of the turbo engines firing up and thrusting the sail sub forwards and then down, under the surface. Bubbles of trapped air raced across the canopy.

It took Max's eyes a moment to adjust to the undersea conditions. Ever since Lia had given him the Merryn Touch he'd had excellent vision under the sea, and now up ahead he could see her form, racing away from him.

Max pushed the thruster control to full power and the sail sub shot after her, pressing him back into the cushioned seat. It took just a few seconds to catch up with the Merryn princess. As Max zoomed beneath her, overtaking, he looked up through the transparent canopy and waved. Lia looked furious. *That's turbo power!*

Rounding the final buoy, Max zipped through the water and pulled back on the steering column. The sail sub burst up through the surface, leapt into the air, and hopped over the finishing line. It splashed down in the shallows, close to the Aquoran shore. Max saw his mother waiting on a boat ramp, lit by lamplights along the waterfront.

"Impressive," she said. "But I thought you said you'd only use wind power in the race?"

"I might have done," Max admitted. Then he grinned. "But what's the point of having a turbo submarine mode, if you can't use it?" He opened the plexiglass canopy, stood and stretched.

The day's light had almost completely gone now and Max looked up at the city itself to see tier after tier of giant skyscrapers rising up to the night sky, electric lights twinkling in countless windows. It was a spectacular scene. Rivet, Max's dogbot, came splashing up to greet him through the waves.

"Max won!" Rivet barked.

Max helped his friend up and into the cockpit of the sail sub just as Lia surfaced. She shook her head and strapped on her Amphibio mask, which allowed her to breathe out of water. The pink glow of the final buoy lit her face and Max could see she was trying to control her temper.

"You cheated!" she complained.

"Yes. Sorry about that," Max said, feeling a little guilty. "But I needed to test the sail sub properly. You're not the only one who can go underwater, you know."

"Well, if we can use anything we like, let's have another race," Lia said. "This time I'll ride Spike. He'll beat any tech you can come up with."

Lia put her fingers to her temples, and Max knew she must be using her Merryn Aqua Powers to call her pet swordfish, Spike. Sure enough, a silvery shape darted through the water. Spike appeared and nuzzled his mistress. Max was about to retort when the light from the buoy went out, plunging them into darkness. Behind him he heard Rivet.

"City dark, Max."

Max spun to see. Rivet was right. It wasn't just the buoy light that had gone out. The lamplights on the waterfront, the window lights in the skyscrapers...even the headlights of the hover cars on the street. They'd all gone out. Aquora was completely dark. *A power cut?*

"What's happening, Max?" Lia called.

Max flicked on the subsail's battery-operated lights as Lia climbed onto Spike's back and moved closer to the gently rocking vessel.

Max's mind was racing. "It must be the power core," he said.

Niobe dived from the pitch black docks and swam effortlessly through the shallows, her pale-green jumpsuit barely visible under the dark waves. Max's mum also had the Merryn Touch, and was just at home in the water as Max was.

"We've had a lot of strange power surges recently," she said, surfacing alongside the sail sub. "And now this blackout… Perhaps the power convertor is malfunctioning."

There's only one way to find out!

"I'm going down to investigate," Max said. He gunned the engine, and Rivet barked.

"Wait for me!" Lia called, swimming up to them on Spike.

"I'd better get to Engineering Headquarters to see if your father needs help," Niobe said. "Be careful down there!"

Max left the sail sub's canopy open as he nosed the vessel under the waves, towards the ocean floor. The Merryn Touch didn't just give him excellent eyesight, it also allowed him to breathe underwater without a mask. As they dived deeper, the sub's lights illuminated the familiar hub of Aquora's power core, a mesh of metal spheres just above the ocean floor, which cooled the power core inside it. A cylindrical column connected the orb to the seabed, and to the city above, carrying energy.

Max felt a shiver down his spine at the awesome sight. His dad had told him how, many hundreds of years ago, Aquoran

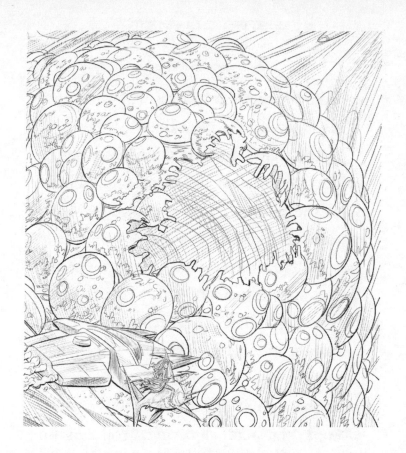

engineers had dug deep into the core of Nemos, drawing heat and pressure up into the power core to be converted into electricity for the city.

Lia pointed ahead. "It looks like it's still damaged from the battle with Gulak," she said. There was a hole of shredded metal, ripped into the mesh spheres.

"Big hole, Max!" Rivet said.

"You're right," Max said grimly. Aquora had recently been attacked by the Robobeast, Gulak the Gulper Eel, commanded by Max's evil cousin Siborg.

As the sail sub came to rest on the ocean floor, Max pushed off and swam towards the cooling spheres at the bottom of the steel shaft, with Lia following on Spike. They passed through the bite hole, careful not to touch the jagged edges.

"Look," Lia said, shivering. "You can see the teeth marks left by Gulak."

But Max had other fears. They swam into the central sphere, where he remembered the orb of the energy converter swirling, pulsing and humming with power. But now it was dark and still.

"It looks like the converter's dead,"

said Max. "That means Aquora has no power at all!"

Lia raised an eyebrow. "You Breathers can get by without tech for a little while, surely?"

Max ran through all the systems that relied on the power core's electricity in his mind. Lights, elevators, hovercars, Water Filtration, Food Storage... He felt panic swirling in his chest, as he turned to Lia. "I don't think so. Without power, Aquora can't survive for more than a week."

CHAPTER TWO

THE FOUR ELEMENTS

A short time later, Max was sitting with Lia and his parents, Niobe and Callum, at a table in the pilot room of the *Sea Hammer*, just off the shores of Aquora. Normally Max would have been thrilled to explore Aquora's prize naval destroyer, and to get a look at the new prototype long range defence torpedo on board. But right now there were more important things to worry about.

"At least the navy vessels still have

power," Niobe said.

The walls were covered with banks of glowing computer monitors and sophisticated instruments. Callum flicked a switch and Max squinted against the light of a hologram. It was a 3D image of the power core. Callum looked worried, tapping the keys on his tablet computer. Seeing his father like this made Max feel even more anxious.

"The converter works by chemical reaction," Max explained to Lia. "There are four rare elements within the orb; Flaric, Magnetese, Blinc and Infernium. Each of them plays a vital role in maintaining the reaction."

"So what's the problem?" Lia asked.

"The elements are unstable," Max said. "Gulak's attack caused a feedback loop which fried the orb, and the elements within it." He waved at the hologram, zooming in and showing Lia close-up images of the four elements as they should have looked; a glimmering, see-through liquid, a fine metal powder, a crystalline solid and a soft metal.

"Can't you just turn it off and on again?" Lia asked. "That's what you Breathers usually do when your 'tech' goes wrong."

"That won't work," Callum told her. He stood, imposing in his black uniform, and waved a hand at the hologram so that it showed the elements as they looked now. Grey, dead, cold. "They might as well be piles of sand for all the good they'll do," he said.

Max swallowed nervously before turning to Lia. "This technology is so advanced we're not entirely sure how to fix it."

Lia tutted. "I can't believe you Breathers built something but then forgot how it works."

"Now hang on..." Max began, feeling his face flush with annoyance.

Niobe put a gentle hand on Max's shoulder.

"There's a lot of old tech we use without being entirely sure how, or even when, it was built," she explained to Lia. "Humans have been on this planet for thousands of years. There have been wars and famines, civilisations have fallen and risen again many times. The old records were destroyed, or lost."

"Which means we'll have to use our own ingenuity to find a way to repair the core," Callum said. "And quickly."

"How much fresh water do we have?" Max asked.

"Seven days' worth," Callum said. "Maybe eight at a push. Then people will start to suffer from dehydration, and soon after that…there will be fatalities."

As he said this, Max felt his mouth go dry, as if he were already feeling the pangs of thirst. *It's a race against time.*

"There'll be food shortages, too," Max's

father went on. "No hovercars, no lights, no heating…there's bound to be chaos. We have to restart that power core."

"To do that, we'll need fresh supplies of the four elements," Niobe said. "They're very rare. In fact, there may not be any left at all."

"Left where?" Max asked.

Niobe looked up at her son, worried. "The only possible place would be far from here," she replied. "In the Primeval Sea."

"Forget it," Callum muttered.

"I've never heard of the Primeval Sea," Lia said.

"That's because no one's ever been there," Callum said, running a hand through his dark hair. "And nothing's ever come from there except old myths." He waved at the hologram and the image changed into a map of the seas, zooming out from Aquora and then the entire Delta Quadrant until it was only a tiny section on the map. Far to the west, the map lacked detail. There was nothing but great blank stretches of ocean.

"This uncharted section is the Primeval Sea," Callum said. "We don't know for sure that the elements can be found there, and it would take much longer than eight days to journey there and back, in any case. Like I said, forget it." Callum and Niobe shared a look of despair that gave Max a sick feeling in his stomach. If even his parents had given up, then surely it was hopeless.

Lia had stood and was inspecting the holomap carefully. "You need to go here?" She asked, pointing to the uncharted section.

"Yes," Callum said. "But it would take two weeks even in the *Nebula X4*, our fastest sub."

Lia grunted in agreement. "The only way to get there quicker would be if you were swept away by the Deep Sea undertow," she said casually. "It flows right past."

"Of course!" Max said. He sat up, suddenly fired with hope. "That's how we can get there. We can ride the undertow." He grinned at the Merryn princess.

"Whoa!" Lia said, holding up her hands. "I wasn't seriously suggesting we try it. Remember the time we fought Silda? The undertow tossed us about like corks."

"And those currents are strong," Callum

said. "Even our toughest battlesub would be torn apart by them."

Max nodded. "But a smaller vessel could harness that strength. If I modified the sail sub..." He flicked on another holoscreen and started sketching with his finger. "Look, I can use the sails underwater to keep the sub stable."

Callum inspected the glowing digital sketch, considering. "It might just work," he said.

It HAS to work. "I could get to the Primeval Sea in less than a day," Max said.

"You're not going without me," Lia said. "We don't know what you'll encounter when you get there, but I bet my Aqua Powers will prove very useful."

"You two do make a great team," Callum said.

"Well, then, I'm coming too," Niobe said.

Max shook his head sadly. "There's no room, Mum. It'll be a squeeze with just me and Lia.

Maybe I can fit Rivet in too, but not an adult. We can't even take Spike with us – he won't survive the undertow."

Lia's eyes dropped. Max knew she would feel sad leaving her pet behind. They'd never been on a Quest without Spike. But they didn't have a choice.

"Max is right," Callum said to Niobe. "Besides, I need you here with me. Someone has to help organise the rationing and keep order in the city."

Niobe still looked concerned, but Max placed his hand over hers and smiled. "Don't worry, Mum," he said. "Lia and I have been on loads of Sea Quests before. We'll bring back those elements. Trust me."

∘ ∘ ∘

Max, Lia and Rivet hurried along the waterfront back to where Max had been modifying the sail sub in the dry docks.

Aquorans milled about, worried looks on their faces as they headed to stores to stock up on provisions.

As they passed one food store, Max saw a scuffle break out when a man tried to jump the queue. A Defence Officer ran to break up the fight.

"There's Max North," one woman cried out, seeing them. "He'll help us!"

Ever since Max had returned from the Chaos Quadrant and saved the city from

Siborg's terrifying mind-bugs, some of the people of Aquora had begun to treat him like a hero. But today Max felt helpless in the face of the mounting panic brought about by the power cut. A siren wailed suddenly, and everyone stopped what they were doing, waiting to hear the announcement. Max felt his chest swell with pride as his father's reassuring voice boomed across the city.

"People of Aquora. Not for the first time, our city is under threat. We have no power, and our supply of fresh water is limited. But it's essential we do not panic, that we work together to get through this crisis. A team headed by my son Max is today heading on a journey to locate and bring back essential elements to repair the power core. We must have faith in him. He has saved the city of Aquora more than once before."

As his father's words echoed, Max could see

people watching him. Most had expressions of trust and support. But he could see doubt in some faces too, and fear.

I can't let them down.

Max hurried to the dry docks and got to work putting finishing touches to the sail sub modification. Earlier, Max had sailed the vessel into one of the small repair slips. Usually, he'd have been able to use the electric pumps to drain the dock of seawater, but because there was no power, he'd had to use a hand-operated winch to lift the sail sub out of the water and swing it over to where he could get underneath it.

Rivet brought Max tools and used his strong jaws to hold things steady. Lia tried to help too, but the Merryn princess wasn't used to Breather tools, and kept mixing up spanners with hammers. In the end they decided it was best if she just let them get on with it.

When he was finally happy, Max flicked the switch to unfurl the spinnaker. The metal sail pointed forwards, with the thin metal sail forming a long cone shape around it like a parachute. It was designed to catch the sea currents coming from behind the vessel, forcing it forwards and giving Max more control, while the sharp nose of the sail would minimise water resistance.

Max was proud of his idea. He opened and closed the sail a number of times, admiring the smooth operation. Lia watched him impatiently from behind her Amphibio mask.

"Very nice," she said wryly. "Let's hope it works better than your power core."

"This vessel just needs one more thing," Max said. "A name."

"I'll never understand why you Breathers insist on naming things which aren't even alive," Lia muttered.

"All ships need a name. I'm going to call it the *Silver Porpoise*."

"Maybe a better name would be the *Silver Tortoise*?" Lia suggested.

"Why?" Max asked.

"Because it's so slow," Lia teased.

Max was about to retort when his parents arrived, each carrying an object. Callum pressed his into Max's hands. It was a round metal container.

"For the elements," Callum explained.

"There are four compartments. Remember the elements are extremely unstable so keep them apart from one another."

Niobe handed a small device to Max. It was a flat tablet with a keypad and a small screen. "It's an energy tracker," Niobe said. "We were using it to monitor the energy surges in the core. I've modified it to help you locate the elements when you get to the Primeval Sea."

"I was going to ask about that," Max said. "How will I know where to find them? Even with the tracker, it'll be like looking for a needle – four! – in a haystack!"

"It might not be quite as difficult as that," Callum said. "The elements should all be found in the same place."

"And where's that?" Lia asked.

Max's parents exchanged a glance before Niobe answered. "Inside the engine of a crashed starship."

CHAPTER THREE

CURRENT SURFING

Max's heart leapt with excitement. *A starship? How…?*

"Remember I told you that humans had been on this planet for thousands of years?" Niobe said. "Well, they – I mean, we – originally arrived here on spaceships."

"Humans are from Outer Space?" Lia asked as Max's eyes widened. "That explains a lot."

"We don't know much about those first brave colonists," Niobe went on, "where they came from, or why they came here. But one thing we do know is that when they arrived, they took apart their spaceships to build cities here on Nemos. Aquora's power core was built using part of the engine from one of those ships."

"That's why we don't know exactly how it works," Callum added, glancing at Lia. "It was built on another planet, for a start."

Over on the waterfront, Max heard the sound of a guard shouting and the raised voices of protesting Aquorans.

"We're already having trouble keeping people calm," Niobe said, her brows knitted.

"The legends say that another spaceship crash-landed in the Primeval Sea," Callum went on. "There are almost certainly others elsewhere on Nemos, too."

"Might there be other cities like Aquora?" Max asked, fascinated.

"Quite probably," Callum said. "What we do know is that the ship in the Primeval Sea, if it's there, should have supplies of the four elements we need to restart our power core."

So what are we waiting for?

With his father's help, Max hauled the crane arm around so the *Silver Porpoise* dangled over the water of the harbour. It was time to go. Max shivered as he thought of the Quest ahead. He hugged his parents, then leapt into the cockpit of the *Silver Porpoise*, followed by Rivet and Lia. It was a tight squeeze.

Will I have enough room to operate the controls? Max slowly fed the winch out until they floated on the surface, then released the cradle. Niobe waved as Callum pressed the control which closed the canopy. As they slipped below the surface the last thing Max saw was the proud but worried faces of his parents. The Quest had begun.

° ° °

"There it is!" Lia cried. "The undertow."

Up ahead, Max saw debris, plants and broken pieces of coral shoot past, carried along at enormous speed by the current. He powered down the turbo engines and the *Silver Porpoise* slowed so they could get a good look at the raging water.

Spike had accompanied them this far and now tapped on the canopy. Lia pressed her hand against the plexiglass, using her Aqua Powers to say goodbye to her friend. Max thought he saw a tear on her cheek.

"I wish you could come with us," Lia said.

"He can't fit in here," Max reminded her, "even if we could fit an Amphibio mask over his sword!" He went to press the thruster control but Lia put a hand on his to stop him.

"Wait! I have a better idea," Lia said.

A few minutes later they were ready. Lia had left the cockpit of the sail sub and was now astride Spike, where she looked a lot more comfortable. A length of rope stretched between them and the *Silver Porpoise*. Lia held on to the rope's triangular handle.

"Are you sure about this?" Max asked.

"It's risky," Lia said through the headset, "but I used to go current skiing all the time when I was little. Not in the undertow, of course... But I just can't leave Spike."

"What about all the debris flying past?' Max asked.

"Your sail should protect us, shouldn't it?" Lia said.

"Yes, I think so," Max said. "OK, to be honest, it was a little cramped in the cockpit!"

"You can say that again," Lia said, stretching her legs out.

Let's roll! Max hit the thrusters again and the *Silver Porpoise* nosed into the undertow. At once, the torrent snatched at them and hurled them along, into the depths. Max had been expecting a bumpy ride but nothing on this scale. He and Rivet were thrown around the cockpit as the sail sub spun crazily among chunks of debris. Max felt panic bubbling up inside him. *What if they never regained control?* He took a deep breath and grabbed hold of the rudder. He needed to stabilise the vessel or else they'd be battered to a pulp. He pressed the button which opened the modified spinnaker and held his breath. *This HAS to work!*

As the sail unfurled, billowing out into a sharp cone shape, it caught the current and wrenched the *Silver Porpoise* along behind it, like a half-opened umbrella catching the wind. Suddenly, Max had control. They were on an even keel again, the hills and gullies of the seabed whizzing by below them.

"Steady, Max!" Rivet barked joyfully.

Max used the flaps to keep the sail sub upright. "Are you OK?" he called out to Lia. He risked a quick look behind to see Spike racing along, the rope taut in Lia's hands.

"We're fine," she yelled, the current roaring through her headset. "This is much better than last time, when we were spun round and

round. As long as I stay within the slipstream, the current is steady."

"Does this mean you're now converted to the wonders of technology?" Max asked.

"I never said that!" Lia snapped back.

"OK. But can you handle a bit more speed?"

"We can handle anything you can throw at us," Lia's voice said in his headset.

Max unfurled the sail more fully, to catch more of the current, and they shot ahead like a startled sailfish. The *Silver Porpoise* was stable now, but the current was still strong and turbulent. Stones and lumps of coral rushed past bouncing off the hard plexiglass canopy. Max had to fight with the controls to avoid the bigger chunks of rock.

Even at such huge speeds, the journey to the Primeval Sea was long. Max began to worry that Lia's arms must be getting tired. He checked on her every half an hour or so.

"We're fine," she said each time, grimly.

Even Max's arms were beginning to ache as he held the controls firm, and his mind was starting to drift. At least Rivet's occasional barks kept him focused.

Max had set up the energy reader so he could check it without taking his hands off the controls. Gradually, painfully slowly, he saw the faint red light of the elements appear on the screen. His heart leapt. He turned around and squinted out of the plexiglass to see Lia hanging on determinedly, surfing along on the wake and careful to stay within the calmer water in the slipstream of the *Porpoise*.

"Nearly there," he called to Lia. "Another ten minutes or so."

"Look, Max!" Rivet barked.

Max spun back to see a huge rock speeding towards them through the murky water. Any second now, they would be crushed!

Adrenaline surged through Max as he hauled on the controls, instinct taking over. The rock was almost on them. Rivet whined.

We're not going to make it!

With a crunch and a scrape the rock hit the side of the *Silver Porpoise*. A shockwave juddered through the frame so hard that Max felt it in his teeth.

"Max!" Lia cried. Behind the sail sub, she was spinning crazily. The rock seemed to

have missed her, but the lurching of the
Silver Porpoise had thrown her off balance.
Max watched in horror as Lia fought to keep
control. She spun to the left and downwards,
out from the calm of the sail sub's slipstream
and into the violent current. The handle of
the rope was torn from her hands and she
shouted out. Max felt a hand clutch his heart
as Lia and Spike went tumbling off into the
undertow.

CHAPTER FOUR

THE PRIMEVAL SEA

Max slammed the controls to the left, following Lia's path down into the murky depths. He could just see her through the debris, clinging desperately to Spike's fin. "Hold on!" he cried. But if Lia heard him he couldn't tell.

More and more material was now flying through the torrent.

They'll be smashed to pieces!

The *Silver Porpoise* ran through a shower

of tiny coral pieces which rattled on the canopy like hailstones. Another, smaller rock bounced off the sail sub's nose with a sharp crack. If the hull was breached, the *Silver Porpoise* would be torn apart, along with Max and Rivet.

Max pushed the thruster lever as the Merryn princess and her swordfish tumbled deeper and deeper through the torrent.

I've got to get to them.

Smaller and lighter than the sail sub, they were quickly being swept away from safety.

"Faster, Max," Rivet barked.

Max flicked a switch and opened the sail further, making it expand like a huge metal umbrella. The *Silver Porpoise* surged forward. More pieces of rock hit the sail with a sound like popping corn. Max knew that if it were damaged, it would leave them without any means of propulsion, but he had to take that risk to save their friends. The *Silver Porpoise* rocked in the torrent but was moving much faster now. It soon overtook Lia and Spike. Max spun the vessel and opened the sail as wide as it would go, shielding them both.

Spike steadied himself in the calmer water and quickly moved over to his mistress who climbed onto his back again. Max saw her hug him tightly. The trailing tow rope swung past and Lia grabbed it gratefully. With the spinnaker fully open Max was struggling to keep the sail sub steady, shifting the angle of the metal sail to keep them balanced.

"Thanks!" Lia said, the sound of her voice crackling slightly in Max's earpiece. They were back in control now and Max closed the sail a little to reduce the chance of damage.

"Phew, that was close," Max said. But his heart lurched again as he realised they were dangerously close to the ocean floor. Rivet barked, gripping the shuddering cockpit seat with his claws. From the darkness loomed the massive wreck of a submarine.

We're heading straight for it!

It was a giant, rusted hulk with tangled rails and a massive, twisted gun barrel. Max

wrenched the controls to one side, missing the wreck by a hair's breadth. But the sudden change in direction sent the *Silver Porpoise* into an uncontrolled spin. A colossal surge in the undertow seized them like a toy and hurled them onwards and down, towards the ocean floor. Max shut his eyes, waiting for the crunch… But it didn't come. Instead, Max felt the sail sub slow suddenly. He and Rivet were thrown forward with a sickening jolt. He opened his eyes and gasped. The *Silver Porpoise* had come to rest in still water, hung all about with wispy clouds which sparkled with a thousand colours.

"Where are we?" Lia asked in wonder. She and Spike seemed to have come out of their tumble without getting hurt.

Max looked down at the energy tracker. The display now showed a cluster of dim red lights. Could those be the elements? But the lights should be brighter, and all together…

"Looks like we've arrived," Max said, puzzled. "This is the Primeval Sea."

"I told you the undertow was fast," Lia said.

Max closed the sail, fired up the turbo engines and moved slowly out from the shimmering cloud into clearer water, exploring their new surroundings. The ocean here seemed different, a milky turquoise lit by thin beams of light filtering down through the cloudy fathoms. Here and there opaque patches hung like fog.

"The water's hot," Lia called as she and Spike passed through one of the foggy patches. "Too hot!" She had let go of the rope now, and was swimming alongside the sub.

Strange fish swam by, looking at Max curiously through the plexiglass. One type had three eyes and brightly-shining scales. Max saw an enormous, glowing jellyfish float past the *Silver Porpoise* , its trailing tentacles sparkling with energy. The creature wobbled along the ocean floor between tendrils of mutated, twisted kelp and glowing boulders.

"Whoa!"

Out of nowhere another large creature sprang from the seabed, snatching at the jellyfish with huge jaws. The jellyfish lurched out of the way and Max saw with amazement that the attacker was anchored to the sea floor, its gaping mouth green and mossy. It was a plant, not an animal.

"What is this place?" Max asked in wonder.

"I don't know," Lia replied. "I thought I knew every sea creature on Nemos. But I've never seen anything like these before."

The *Silver Porpoise* moved on, with Lia and Spike keeping pace alongside. Max steered between sharp towers of rock jutting from the seabed like giant blades. The tops of some of them gave off an unearthly glow.

Max peered at the screen of the tracker. "The signal's spread out," he said over the intercom. "There's more than one reading. Lots of faint patches of high energy."

"What does that mean?" Lia asked.

"I don't know," Max said. "But I'm worried that the elements may have leaked out into the surrounding ocean from the starship's engine. Maybe that's what's causing these weird mutations in the local sea-life."

"Technology!" Lia snorted.

"Let's just hope there's enough left in the ship for our needs," Max said. "I'm heading towards one of the strongest readings." They crested an enormous pinnacle of rock and Max's jaw dropped open.

The starship!

"So big, Max!" Rivet barked.

The dogbot was right. Up ahead, in a deep

trench, lay the colossal hulk of a crashed ship. It looked to be roughly the size of one of the bigger Aquoran skyscrapers, but as it was partially buried in the silt, it may have been larger still. The ship's hull seemed mostly intact, if twisted and corroded.

"Imagine it," Max said breathlessly. "This brought some of the first people to Nemos."

"It is pretty impressive, I suppose," Lia said.

"I wonder where they went," Max went on. "Did they found some city like Aquora?" He was about to move closer when a shadow passed across the plexiglass, then another. Max looked up to see two huge shapes heading straight towards them, fast. As they came closer, he got a better view. Uh oh.

"Sharks!" Lia cried, pulling Spike around and holding out her spear.

These were some of the biggest and weirdest sharks Max had ever seen. They

were long and sleek, like they were built for speed. They had thin fins and tails, and their mouths were huge, filled with so many sword-like teeth they seemed unable to close.

"I'm using my Aqua Powers to talk to them," Lia said, "but they're not responding."

"Watch out, Lia!" Rivet barked as one of the sharks raced towards her, jaws snapping.

Lia and Spike darted out of the way, only

for the shark to follow. Max's chest tightened with fear as he saw the second shark coming straight for the *Silver Porpoise*.

The sharks are on the attack!

CHAPTER FIVE

WELCOME ABOARD

The first shark went after Lia and Spike, who zipped away. Meanwhile the second was closing on the *Silver Porpoise*. Max flipped some switches on the weapon control panel, setting torpedoes to stun, and fired one. The torpedo fizzed away from them, arcing upwards towards the attacking shark. But with a quick flip of a fin, the shark twisted gracefully and dodged the torpedo with astonishing agility.

"Shark too fast, Max!" Rivet barked.

Max gasped as the huge fish battered into the sail sub with its stubby nose. Max and Rivet were thrown from their feet as the vessel's frame groaned under the impact. As Max got up, he saw that the shark had seized the hull with its huge jaws. He heard the screeching of the sub's plating as the animal's

massive teeth dug into it.

What kind of creature is this? Now the shark was so close, Max could see a strange, flashing light on the side of its head, clearly man-made. A terrible thought struck him. Had the poor shark been altered robotically? *But how is that possible, without the Professor or Siborg...?* Thinking quickly, he flipped open the metal spinnaker. The unfurling sail shoved the shark backwards and away from the sail sub. It seemed surprised and Max took his chance, firing a second torpedo. This time the missile exploded against the shark's flank with a flash of light, a sharp crack and a visible shockwave that shook the *Silver Porpoise* with its force.

As Max's eyes readjusted, he saw the shark drifting to the bottom of the sea, stunned, waving its tail weakly. Max scanned the ocean for the shark that had been chasing Lia and

Spike. He saw it had cornered them against a rocky outcrop. Lia took a swipe at the monster with her spear, but it dodged the strike, flipped around and smashed its powerful tail into Spike. Lia was sent tumbling. Spike seemed to have been knocked unconscious. He drifted, spinning lazily.

The shark swam straight towards Lia, bearing down on her...

"Shark eat Lia, Max!" Rivet said.

We'll see about that.

Max slammed his hand down on the torpedo control. Another stun torpedo fizzed out of the tube and rocketed towards the shark.

"Hit, Max, HIT!" Rivet barked as the torpedo slammed into the shark, exploding in a bright blast and releasing a cloud of bubbles. As they cleared, Max's heart sank to see the shark was still moving, and coming again for Lia. Its cruel teeth shone white and Lia held up a hand in desperation as it reached her and opened its jaws wide…

Max powered the thrust lever forward, and the sail sub raced through the water. But it wasn't fast enough. *We're not going to get there in time!*

At the last moment, a silver shape flashed into view. *Spike!* The swordfish had recovered. Lia hooked a hand around his dorsal fin and he towed her away, racing to safety. As the shark came after them, Max fired one more torpedo, hitting the shark right on the nose. This time the massive animal went rigid and floated down towards the sea floor, unconscious.

They were safe, but Max's whole body was shaking.

That was close. Too close.

"I've never seen sharks like that before!" Lia gasped as she and Spike swam up to the *Silver Porpoise*. "Why couldn't I speak to them?"

"I think they were Robobeasts," Max said. "I saw a bleeping light on one of them."

"So, mini-Robobeasts now?" Lia said. "Who could be behind this? A human, I bet."

"We need to clear this area," Max said, "in case those sharks recover." He nosed the *Silver Porpoise* closer to the starship that was looming over them in the pale-blue water.

"What's that red coating on the sides?" Lia asked.

"Rust," Max said. "This thing has been here a long time."

"Looks like it's only the barnacles that are holding it together," Lia said.

They cruised over the top of the ship and Max saw that its main body section was circular, like a plate. It was dotted with portholes, many of them broken. Max saw an eel slip into one as they approached. Beyond the main body, the ship tapered out into a long tail. Max felt his chest swell in awe.

This starship is just…huge!

"What are those tube things stuck on the tail?" Lia asked.

"Thrusters," Max replied. A couple were broken off and lying, half-buried in the sand, but there were four still attached, running alongside the ship's tail, each as long as an Aquoran battle cruiser. Even Lia seemed impressed with the scale of it.

"Come on," said Max as he anchored the sub to the hull of the starship. "We need to get those elements from the engine, fast." He gathered his hyperblade, the container for the elements and the energy tracker. Then he and Rivet exited the sail sub and swam to the starship's hull. "Considering how many portholes are broken, the entire ship must be flooded," Max said.

"Stay here," Lia told Spike. "Guard the *Silver Tortoise* – I mean, *Porpoise*!"

Max swam into the wreck through one of the broken portholes, careful not to cut himself on the remaining glass, which was at least half a metre thick. This was nothing like the windshield on his aquabike! His eyes adjusted to the gloom as he waited for Lia and Rivet to catch him up. A creeping sensation washed over him as shapes started to form in the dark.

No one's been on this deck for more than two thousand years!

It was hard to tell the original purpose of the chamber but it may have been a café or mess hall. There was a long counter on one side and scattered mounds all about which may once have been tables and chairs. Everything was covered with barnacles, coral and kelp. Tiny fish flitted about.

"It's deserted," Lia said behind him. "Creepy."

Rivet disappeared behind the counter and came back carrying an object which he gave to Max.

"It's a spoon," Max said, scraping away the barnacles. "Made of some rust-proof material." Seeing such an everyday object here made him feel closer to the brave pioneers who'd arrived on this ship, and had chatted and eaten in this room. Max shivered.

Somehow it feels like this ship isn't dead, just sleeping.

They moved out of the room through doors that must have been electronic once, into a second chamber. This one had some objects which looked as though they might have once been beds. Counters ran around the walls, teeming with sea-life.

"The hospital?" Max guessed aloud. A little crab with too many legs scuttled across the floor as Max approached to investigate.

"There's no one here eith—" Lia began, but was interrupted by a bark from Rivet.

Max looked up. "Wait!" he said, pointing to the far corner where Rivet was facing. Max thought he'd seen something small, darting along by the ceiling. "What was that?"

"What was what?" Lia asked. "I don't see anything."

"It looked like a little metal device. Round, like a ball..."

"Are you sure you weren't just imagining

it?" Lia asked. "Or maybe it was a fish?"

Max frowned. Were his eyes playing tricks? He just couldn't shake the feeling that something else was on board with them.

They carried on, swimming down a long, curving corridor until they came to a much larger set of doors, half-closed. Max squeezed through, followed closely by Lia and Rivet. They found themselves in a huge space, like an Aquoran factory, filled with robotic machines fixed to the floor. Vehicles and cranes littered the deck.

"I'm guessing these are the engineering docks," Max said. "There's something different about this room, though."

"Maybe it's just that there's something in it," Lia said, inspecting a nearby piece of machinery. She pulled at a lever and an arm swung around, causing her to duck. "Whoa! This seems operational, anyway."

"That's it!" Max said. "In the other rooms, everything was covered with sea-life. These machines are clean and in working order."

Someone's been using them.

"You are correct," said a new voice behind them.

CHAPTER SIX

IRIS

Max spun round, unsheathing his hyperblade. But the room was empty.

"It sounded like...like a girl," Lia said. "A young, human girl."

"Again, you are correct," the voice answered. This time, Max realised where it was coming from – speakers on the wall, muffled slightly by the water, but clear enough to make it seem like there was someone in the room with them. "Welcome to the starship *Liberty*," the voice said. Rivet growled.

"Hush, Rivet," Max said. "Who are you?"

"My name is Iris," the girl replied. Something about her voice made the hair on Max's arms stand on end.

"Did you discover the wreck too?" he asked. "How are you talking to us through the speakers?"

"Come back out into the corridor and follow it along to the end," the girl replied. "I'm waiting for you there."

"I don't like this," Lia whispered to Max.

"Me neither," Max muttered back. "But we have to investigate."

Whoever she is, and whatever she's doing here, maybe Iris can help us find the elements.

They set off down the long corridor, which curved slowly, following the shape of the starship's forward section. Eventually it opened out into a chamber even more massive than the engineering docks. Max gasped as he looked up.

In the centre of the chamber, anchored to

both floor and ceiling by huge girders, was a colossal metal sphere connected to a shaft, rising to the ceiling.

"The engine!" Max cried. Then his attention was drawn to what surrounded it. All around the walls of the circular chamber were rows of pods, with open doors. Max inspected one. Inside was a seat, cracked and infested with sea-life, tubes hanging down within the compartment, moving in the slight current.

"Cryogenic pods," Max said. "They must have carried the crew, the first settlers on Nemos. Empty for centuries."

"There's no sign of Iris," Lia said, looking around the vast space. Max saw that she clenched her spear tightly in both hands. He crossed the chamber to inspect the engine.

"The shape of it," Lia said. "It looks like…"

"The housing of Aquora's energy core," Max finished. "They could be twins. Look, there's a

section missing here." Someone, or something, had removed a heavy metal plate and left it lying on the ground. Max peered through the gap. It was dark inside. He held out his energy tracker. "The readings are faint," he said. "No different from how they were outside."

"The reactor is non-functional," the girl's voice said suddenly.

Max jumped and turned to see that a nearby vidscreen had flickered into life. It was filled by a girl's face with flashing green eyes. She

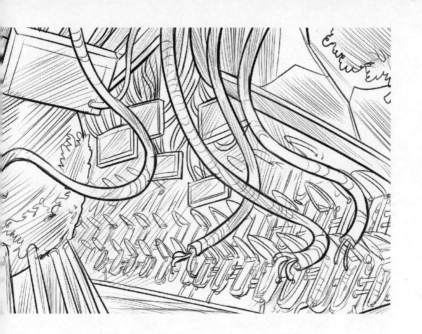

looked Aquoran, and about Max's age.

"Iris," he said. "Who are you, and how did you get here?"

"I've always been here," Iris replied. "Ever since the crash."

"But that was thousands of years ago," Lia said. "All the pods are empty."

"The people who were in the pods left the ship," Iris said, sadly. "They went off to colonise the planet…they abandoned me!" Her voice suddenly grew angry, and for an instant the

image on the screen flickered red.

Questions crowded Max's mind, but Iris spoke again first. "Who are you?" she asked. "You both breathe underwater, yet it is clear you are different species."

"I am Max, from the city of Aquora in the Delta Quadrant," Max replied. "This is Lia, a Merryn from the city of Sumara."

"It is right that you speak for her," Iris said.

"She is clearly from an inferior species. Is she your slave, perhaps?"

"Now you just listen to me—" Lia began.

"Give me the coordinates of your home cities," Iris demanded, leaving Lia open-mouthed and fuming. Rivet growled again and Max's fears increased. It seemed a strange request. He decided to ignore it.

"We are here to search for rare elements to restart the power core that provides energy to our civilisation," Max said. "We had hoped to find replacement elements here, but the core is empty. Do you know what has happened to the elements?"

"Stolen," Iris said quickly. "The elements within the engine were taken by hostile local scavengers. There are many threats in this ocean. It is my job to protect the ship. React and defend!" Again, the girl's image flickered red. Max narrowed his eyes thoughtfully.

The screen changes colour when she is angry.

"Something about her story doesn't add up," Max muttered to Lia. "She can't have just woken up. The pods are rusted and filled with sea-life."

"You should know," Lia replied frostily. "You are the superior life form after all."

"Life form… That's it!" Max said. "Iris isn't a life form at all."

"What do you mean?" Lia asked.

"She hasn't just come out of a pod, because she was never in one. She didn't leave the ship with the others because she can't."

"You're not making any sense," Lia said.

"Iris is the ship's computer," Max said.

"Correct once more," Iris said. "I am the Intelligent Reactive Interference System. IRIS."

"You've been here, alone, all this time?" Lia asked. Max could hear sympathy in her voice now. The Merryn were a sociable species. The thought of being alone so long must be hard for

Lia to understand. Max walked closer to the screen. It looked old and was slightly cracked.

"I have kept the ship safe since then," Iris replied. "Until the local threats stole the elements. Now it seems I have failed. Without the power core, I have no weapons, no armies, no body to go after the thieves."

"So the elements can be recovered?" Max asked. He thought of his parents back in Aquora, fighting to keep order. *I can't fail.*

"Perhaps," Iris said, after a pause. The face on the vidscreen looked thoughtful. "You must travel to the city of Athalar. That is where the closest element – the Flaric – has been taken."

"Where is Athalar?" Lia asked.

"Not far," Iris replied. "Due north of here. If you bring back the Flaric, you can take some of it for your energy core. There should be more than enough for both our needs."

"No time to lose," Max said. "Let's go!"

CHAPTER SEVEN

THREATS

"This bright spot on the energy reader," Max said, jabbing a finger down on the screen. "This must be the Flaric." He and Rivet were back in the *Silver Porpoise*, racing at full speed away from the starship. Max still couldn't shake the uneasiness he'd been feeling since meeting Iris. An artificially intelligent computer. That kind of technology was far beyond anything in Aquora. But what would centuries and centuries of isolation do to an intelligent mind?

Lia rode alongside on Spike, easily able to keep up with the sail sub. A shoal of mutated fish swam by. Their heads seemed to be upside down, with bulbous eyes where their jaws should have been. Max swerved gently to avoid one of the vicious plants as it reached up towards them, snapping its great jaws.

"I have a bad feeling about this," Lia said. "I don't like this place. And I don't trust Iris."

"She's a little strange, I'll grant you," Max said. "But the energy reader seems to back up her story that the Flaric is close by."

Iris had been right when she'd said Athalar wasn't far. Sure enough, after only a couple of minutes they could see the underwater city looming up ahead, half-hidden behind one of the strange underwater fogs.

"Watch out for any of those hostile locals Iris talked about," said Max.

Rivet peered through the plexiglass, as

Max raised the power on his torpedoes, the launchers humming beneath the vessel.

The city seemed to be made of large blocks of carved stone and was almost as big as Sumara. The buildings were constructed differently, though. Max saw towers of various heights with flat tops rising higgledy-

piggledy from a valley surrounded by jagged spears of rock. There were small, one-storey houses with rounded roofs, and larger buildings too. Some of them had human-sized doors and windows, but others had massive entrances.

"It's completely deserted," said Lia, gliding through the empty stone streets on Spike.

Rivet sniffed. "No one here, Max."

"What could have made all these people leave?" Max asked, aiming his lights into the dark buildings. He parked the *Silver Porpoise* at ground level in a large square in the city. In the exact centre of the square rose a huge, tall, shining monolith – a tower of stone.

"This looks like crystal," Lia said, circling around it on Spike.

Light from the glowing bank of fog reflected off the monolith, twinkling in eerie colours which danced across the rough paving stones of the square. There was no one to be seen as Max left the sub, taking the box his father had given him, the energy reader and his hyperblade. Rivet whirred along beside him and Lia hovered nearby, holding Spike steady. Max shivered, despite the water's warmth.

"Scary, Max," Rivet said as Max swam slowly toward a nearby house, its single door and two windows dark as a tomb. Maybe the element was trapped in one of these buildings.

Movement caught Max's eye and he turned and looked up to see a large shape emerging from one of the cavernous hangars on the far side of the square.

"Something's coming!" shouted Lia.

Max saw a twisting, dark form appear, impossibly huge. He was squinting to get a better look when an intensely bright light shone from it, and he had to shield his eyes.

"Light, Max!" Rivet barked. "Blind."

Just as suddenly, the light went out.

Lia gasped, her eyes clearly recovering quicker than Max's. "It's a...a vampire squid. But it's a robot!"

As Max's vision returned, he saw a colossal metal creature looming over the city. As long as a battlesub, it glinted dully in the glow of the fog. Max saw steel-plated tentacles the length of a ship, each tipped with razor-sharp blades. The tentacles were webbed with some

synthetic material, forming a huge half-sphere. Lights were embedded all along each tentacle. That must be what caused the bright glare, Max realised. Built into the body of the beast were four swivelling energy cannons. The squid waited, its tentacles spiralling, holding position. It made no move to attack.

"It's a Robobeast," Max said hoarsely.

"But who made it?" Lia asked. "And why is it here?"

"I don't know," Max replied, "But I think it's time we got back in the *Silver Porpoise*." Max and Rivet scrambled their way back inside the sail sub. Lia and Spike took up position behind the vessel just as one of the Robobeast's lights blinked into life, projecting a large hologram of a girl's head, hovering about the square before them.

"Iris!" Lia cried.

Iris's oversized head glared at them, her green eyes flashing.

"You are correct," Iris said. "But I don't think you've been introduced to my friend Veloth here. It is a colossal vampire squid – one of my four proudest creations."

"You sent us here, knowing this Robobeast would be waiting for us," Max said. "Why?"

"When I said I have no army," Iris replied coldly, "I wasn't telling the truth. Veloth is my army – along with three other

robotic creations."

Fear squirmed in Max's gut. *Four Robobeasts!*

"I have other weapons too," Iris continued, "made from the local resources."

Max was hit by a sickening thought. "Those robo-sharks," Max said. "They were your doing."

"I call them my defence bots," Iris said. "My soldiers. They help to protect the *Liberty*."

"Only because you're forcing them to fight for you," Lia cried angrily. "You must have used some kind of electronic device to enslave them. We saw the flashing lights."

"The local mutated fauna of the Primeval Sea come in useful," Iris said.

Veloth suddenly shifted, coming closer, and Iris's hologram wobbled for a moment as the projector light mounted on the Robobeast readjusted. Rivet growled as Max felt fear grip his stomach.

"You don't need an army," Max said. "You don't need to hurt us."

"You refused to reveal the location of your cities," Iris replied, the hologram flickering slightly in the cloudy water. "How else was I to force the information from you?"

"And why did you want the information?" Max asked. "So you could send Robobeasts to attack Aquora and Sumara?"

"That is correct," Iris replied. "All threats must be terminated!" Her projection flashed an angry red.

Max swallowed nervously. Could a computer go crazy?

Veloth moved forward again, and Max realised he had to keep her talking.

I have to buy us more time.

"You told us your duty was to protect the *Liberty*," he said. "You're a defence system, you shouldn't be attacking your friends."

Iris flashed red again. "I have no friends. Only threats. Like you and your cities."

"She's paranoid," Max said to Lia. "Maybe there's corrosion in her circuits too. She must have removed the elements from the energy core herself, to power the Robobeasts. That's why the energy tracker led us right to Veloth."

"And now she wants to destroy our homes!" Lia said.

Still flickering red, Iris's projection shouted, "YOU WILL GIVE ME THE COORDINATES!"

"Never," Max replied, his heart thumping with determination. Iris's hologram flashed red one more time, then disappeared.

And the Robobeast attacked.

The vampire squid pulsed through the water, heading straight towards them, tentacles first, spinning and lashing in a deadly whirl. One tentacle smashed into a stone tower and sent great blocks sailing down towards them. Max hit the thrusters and shot out of the way just in time as the blocks came raining down, thumping into the stones of the square. A razor-sharp blade sliced through the water just ahead of the sail sub and Max had to dodge again.

As he righted the *Silver Porpoise*, he saw Lia streak up on Spike, her spear at the ready.

She waited for the right moment, getting up close to the squid, ducking and diving just out of reach of the thrashing tentacles. Max saw her hurl the spear.

"Hit, Max!" Rivet barked, and Max's hopes surged.

But his heart sank as he saw the spear bounce harmlessly off the steel body of the Robobeast. *How can we defeat this creature?*

Max gunned the engines and swerved to avoid one of Veloth's tentacles as it whipped past them, razor edges gleaming cruelly. He saw Lia snatch up her spear and race away. The squid turned towards her and opened fire with its four cannons, sending brilliant white energy bolts zipping past the dodging Merryn girl. Max saw one of the beams hit the tall crystal tower in the middle of the square, causing it to wobble precariously. Even the reflection from the tower was blinding.

"It's the Flaric," Max said over the intercom as he yanked at the controls to avoid another flailing tentacle. "Iris must have used the element to super-power the squid. Flaric burns more brightly than any other element."

The squid moved again, diving towards Lia, faster than Max would have imagined possible. "Watch out, Lia," he said, powering the sub in between his friend and the beast.

He stopped, increased the torpedoes' power and adjusted the sights. Veloth spread its webbed tentacles into a shape like the *Silver Porpoise's* underwater sail. Max was about to fire when he was suddenly blinded by another brilliant white light.

"Can't see, Max!" shouted Rivet.

Neither could Max. He flinched away from the control panel, completely helpless.

"Move, Max," came Lia's desperate voice in his headset. "Veloth is bringing its cannons to bear!"

But with the light still pouring into the cockpit, Max couldn't even see the controls, let alone operate them. He heard a whining sound as Veloth's cannons finished charging and prepared to fire again. *The Silver Porpoise is a sitting duck!*

CHAPTER EIGHT

FLARIC!

"Now, Max," Lia cried again. "Move!"

Max lurched forward, crashing into the controls and slamming his fist down on where he thought the thrusters must be. Instead, he hit the lever which operated the sail. It flipped open with a grinding noise, unfurling completely and blocking out the hideous light from the squid. Max blinked. He could see again. There's the rudder. There's the thruster. In a blink he'd powered up the engines and raced out of the way, into the winding streets of the city.

Glancing quickly behind him he saw Veloth following, twisting and turning, crashing buildings aside if the way got too narrow. Max steered the sail sub through an archway, hoping to trap the squid, but when he turned again he saw the colossal Robobeast simply smash it to pieces in pursuit.

"Lia," Max called. "I need you to distract the squid, to give me enough time to fire my torped—"

"Watch out, Max!" Lia interrupted. Max looked up to see a bladed tentacle slicing down towards the sub.

It's going to hit!

But Lia streaked across on Spike and jammed her spear deep into a joint between two sections of the tentacle. The tentacle recoiled, flicking out at Lia, but missed, smashing into one of the stone houses and sending rocks tumbling. Veloth kept racing after the *Silver Porpoise*. Max twisted in his seat to watch as Lia came around and took aim at another tentacle. But the squid had too many. A third smacked hard into Lia and Spike, sending them spinning away.

"Rivet!" Max said. "You need to cause a distraction."

Rivet didn't need to be told twice. He shot out of the airlock like a four-legged torpedo and fizzed through the water. Max watched carefully as Rivet shot past Veloth's huge eyes. The vampire squid paused and swivelled his massive head to follow the dogbot. Max took his chance. He reversed the thrusters, turning the sail sub quickly to face the Robobeast. He peered through the targeting system, trying

to find a good shot at the distracted squid.

But Veloth didn't follow Rivet. Obviously it didn't think a small robot could be a threat.

Instead Veloth turned back towards Max and the *Silver Porpoise*. Max reached out to fire a torpedo but was knocked out of his seat as one of the squid's tentacles slapped the side of the sail sub. Hauling himself up again on the control panel, Max heard a whining noise as the Robobeast's energy cannon charged up, then a *zzzzap!* as it fired. The *Silver Porpoise* was hit by two bolts of energy, juddering through the frame and shaking Max's body. Max grasped the thruster controls and jammed them forward to escape. Nothing happened.

It's dead!

The sail sub dropped quickly down to the seabed, bouncing off a jagged rock, throwing Max across the cockpit and knocking the air from his lungs as it finally settled, motionless.

Max groaned. I really need to install some seatbelts.

When he looked up, he saw the Robobeast looming over the helpless craft. Veloth's lights dimmed a little as its energy cannon charged up for another, final blast. And as the glare died, Max saw a metal box strapped to the side of the squid's head, like a battery pack. *That must be where the Flaric is*, he thought. There was no way of getting to it, though. There was no escape at all.

"You're trapped," Iris's voice rang out from speakers somewhere on the Robobeast. "Veloth's cannons will blast you to pieces. Tell me the coordinates of your home cities and I will let you live."

"If you kill me," cried Max, "you will never discover Aquora's location!"

"I don't need you," Iris replied. "There is

your slave, the Merryn girl. She will tell me the coordinates. You are expendable."

The bright lights on the squid flared up again as the Robobeast's cannons finished charging. But the delay had allowed Max to get his breath back. He scrambled to his feet and slammed his hand down on the controls, hoping that power might have returned. In his panic, he hit the control for the canopy. It opened up, releasing a torrent of warm water which slammed into his chest, knocking the breath from him again. All the while, he could hear the whining sound of Veloth's fully-charged energy cannons.

A brilliant white light dazzled him and Max put up a protective hand. But it was too late – he was completely blinded. *This is it. This is the end…* he thought as Veloth opened fire. Then a dark shadow flitted across his blurred vision and he felt a firm grip on his aquasuit.

The next moment he was dragged from the *Silver Porpoise*. A shockwave slammed into him from behind and he was hit with the stench of burnt metal and plastic as the sail sub was pounded by the cannon beams.

Max looked up to see who his saviour was. "Rivet!" he cried. "Well done, boy!"

The dogbot's propellers whirred as he carried Max away from the sail sub, gripping Max's aquasuit in his mouth, before letting him go. There was another flash of movement to Max's left. He made out Lia riding Spike, holding her spear. "You okay, Max?"

"Yeah. Thanks to Rivet." *But what about the* Silver Porpoise... *Is it destroyed?*

Max turned to see the squid approaching again. It was between them and the *Silver Porpoise* now. Max and Rivet darted down into the buildings of the city, looking for cover, followed by Lia and Spike. In the distance, Max saw the crystal tower in the town square where they'd first set down. It was damaged and leaning badly, probably thanks to a hit from one of Veloth's energy beams. One good shove, and it would fall. The tower glinted with the lights of the pursuing squid.

Wait – the lights...

"That's it!" Max cried. "I know how to defeat the Robobeast!"

"Would you like to share?" Lia replied as the squid's energy beams zipped past them, boiling the water.

Max pointed to the tower. "We have to use Veloth's own power against it," he said.

Lia's eyes widened as she understood. "Got it!"

Max gripped Rivet tightly as the Robodog took him down to the base of the tower. They stood with their backs to the crystal, facing the approaching Robobeast.

"Go to the top, boy," Max told Rivet. "Wait for my order, then shove as hard as you can."

Rivet barked and then obeyed.

We'll see what a threat my dogbot can be!

Lia clambered off her pet swordfish. "You help too, Spike!"

The swordfish swam away after Rivet. Once more, Veloth loomed over the square, aiming its hideous cannon at them, fully charged again. Max heard the whining that signalled the Robobeast was about to fire. Any moment now, its lights would blaze and it would all be over.

"If this doesn't work, we'll be fried like seaweed cakes," Lia said.

"Then let's hope it does work," Max said grimly.

CHAPTER NINE

THE QUEST CONTINUES

"Close your eyes!" Max shouted. He clenched his own tightly shut, just in time. His eyelids glowed bright red as Veloth unleashed another blinding glare. But this time, the light went away almost immediately, and was followed by a hideous roar from the Robobeast. It sounded like the seabed itself was cracking open.

Max opened his eyes and saw that the first part of his plan had worked. The reflection of the lights against the crystal tower had blinded Veloth. The squid thrashed in anger and confusion as it drifted towards them and came down on the square.

"Wait for it, wait for it…" Lia muttered.

"Now!" Max shouted.

Above them, Rivet shoved, the propellers in his four legs working overtime. Spike lent his power too, pushing his head against the crystal. At last the massive shard of rock shifted. Slowly at first, it began to fall through the water, gradually picking up speed.

Come on… willed Max.

CRASH! Max and Lia dived out of the way just in time, as the crystal tower smashed down onto Veloth. The seabed bucked, throwing up a cloud of silt and sand which glittered in the fog light.

Max and Lia climbed to their feet. As the cloud slowly cleared, they saw the tower in

pieces, half burying the colossal squid. Its twisting tentacles were still moving weakly. They could see one of its great, glowing eyes, blinking at them, defeated. As they stood and stared, the light in its robotic eye faded and died. At last the tentacles stopped moving and came to rest on the stones of the square.

We defeated it!

Max felt relief flood through his body. But he knew the job wasn't quite done. He kicked hard and swam up and over the squid's body, heading for the battery pack he'd seen earlier. Rivet and Lia followed.

"Help me open this," Max asked. Rivet's strong jaws cracked the lid and Max hauled it open to see a fist-sized capsule half-full of a fine white powder. Tubes linked it to the squid's circuitry.

"That's it?" Lia asked, amazed. "That little pile of sand powered this huge monster?"

Max gazed at the capsule, shaking his head in wonder and admiration. "Along with the other four elements, this much Flaric has provided enough power to run Aquora for hundreds of years," he said. "Not to mention the energy it took to hurl a starship across the galaxy to begin with."

Max grabbed the capsule and pulled it out carefully. He could transfer the powder to his father's container when he found somewhere dry to work. Lia, Spike and Rivet swam with

him over to the wreck of the *Silver Porpoise.*

Can it be repaired?

They inspected it. The cockpit was blackened and buckled and there were dents and scorch marks all down one side of the vessel. Nervously, Max opened a maintenance hatch to peer into the engine compartment.

"Do you know," Max said after a moment, "the damage isn't as bad as I'd thought."

"You think you can fix it?" Lia asked.

"I'm sure I can," Max said.

Lia patted the side of the sail sub with a smile. "Maybe the *Silver Porpoise* is better built than I gave her credit for," she said.

"Hey," he said. "You used her real name!"

"I think she's earned it," Lia said.

"The engine's sound," Max said. "Once it's powered up the thrusters will get us moving."

"Moving where?" Lia asked.

"To find the other three elements," Max replied. He held up the energy tracker to show Lia the screen. There were three more red lights, showing strong energy readings. One of them was quite close.

"Iris will try to stop us," Lia said as Max took a tool box from the sail sub's luggage compartment. "I thought we'd seen the last Robobeast after Siborg was imprisoned and the Professor swallowed by Gulak. But Iris? She's a whole new kind of enemy."

"You're right," Max said, tightening some bolts. "A super-intelligent computer system, with access to ancient technologies beyond anything we have on Aquora… No wonder that Robobeast was so powerful."

"She said there are three more of them," Lia said, turning to look out into the foggy waters of the Primeval Sea. "Looks like this Quest is going to be harder than we'd thought."

Spike nuzzled against her shoulder, clearly sensing her concern.

"We can't turn back now," Max said, dropping the spanner back into the tool box and selecting another. "The people of Aquora are counting on us."

"Who said anything about turning back?" Lia asked. "If anyone can recover the other three elements, it's us!"

Max grinned at his friend. He was glad he had her beside him, as well as Spike and Rivet too. Together, they could do anything.

"Now, hurry up and fix the *Silver Porpoise*," Lia told him impatiently. "We have a Quest to complete!"

Don't miss Max's next Sea Quest adventure,

when he faces

GLENDOR
THE STEALTHY SHADOW

Look out for all the books in
Sea Quest Series 8:

THE LORD OF ILLUSION

GORT THE DEADLY SNATCHER

FANGOR THE CRUNCHING GIANT

SHELKA THE MIGHTY FORTRESS

LOOSEJAW THE NIGHTMARE FISH

OUT IN AUGUST 2016!

Don't miss the
BRAND NEW
Special Bumper Edition:

REPTA
THE SPIKED BRUTE

OUT IN JUNE 2016

WIN AN EXCLUSIVE
GOODY BAG

In every Sea Quest book the Sea Quest logo is
hidden in one of the pictures. Find the logos in books
25-28, make a note of which pages they appear on and
go online to enter the competition at

www.seaquestbooks.co.uk

Each month we will put all of the correct entries into a draw
and select one winner to receive a special Sea Quest goody bag.

You can also send your entry on a postcard to:

Sea Quest Competition, Orchard Books,
Carmelite House, 50 Victoria Embankment,
London, EC4Y 0DZ

Don't forget to include your name and address!

GOOD LUCK

Closing Date: May 31st 2016

IF YOU LIKE SEA QUEST, YOU'LL LOVE BEAST QUEST!

Series 1: COLLECT THEM ALL!

An evil wizard has enchanted the magical beasts of Avantia. Only a true hero can free the beasts and save the land. Is Tom the hero Avantia has been waiting for?

FERNO
THE FIRE DRAGON

978 1 84616 483 5

SEPRON
THE SEA SERPENT

978 1 84616 482 8

ARCTA
THE MOUNTAIN GIANT

978 1 84616 484 2

TAGUS
THE HORSE MAN

978 1 84616 486 6

NANOOK
THE SNOW MONSTER

978 1 84616 485 9

EPOS
THE FLAME BIRD

978 1 84616 487 3

DON'T MISS THE
BRAND NEW SERIES OF:

Series 16: THE SIEGE OF GWILDOR

978 1 40833 986 2

978 1 40833 996 1

978 1 40833 988 6

978 1 40833 994 7

COMING SOON